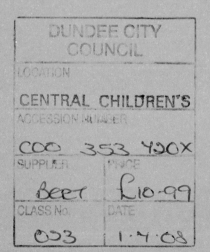

A Day with Dad

Bo R. Holmberg   illustrated by Eva Eriksson

WALKER BOOKS
AND SUBSIDIARIES
LONDON · BOSTON · SYDNEY · AUCKLAND

Tim is waiting on the platform at the train station. He's just moved to this town. He lives here with his mum. His dad lives in another town. But today Tim's dad is coming on the train. They are going to spend the whole day together – just Tim and Dad.

The train pulls into the station and comes to a stop. It sighs, as if it's tired from its long journey. Then the door sighs open – and there's Dad!

As Mum says goodbye, Dad gives Tim a hug and lifts him into the air.

"Hello, Tim!" he says. "What shall we do today?"

Tim knows. He knows what they should do.

On the main street, there's a little stand where you can buy hot dogs. This is where Tim stops.

"Two hot dogs, please," says Dad.

"This is my dad," Tim tells the hot dog lady.

"Where to now, Tim?" Dad says when they've finished their hot dogs.

"Let's go to the cinema!" says Tim, and he shows Dad the way. There's an animated film in five minutes.

"You like animated films, don't you?" says Dad.

Tim nods *yes*.

Tim hands over the tickets at the door. The usher has a big moustache. "Dad and I are going to watch the film," Tim tells him.

Tim and Dad find seats near the middle – Tim always likes to sit in the middle. The film makes Dad laugh. He has a funny laugh. When Tim hears Dad laugh, it makes him laugh too.

When the lights come up, Dad says, "Time for pizza!"

Tim takes Dad to his favourite pizza place. It's called "Santana's" and it's not far from the cinema. The waiter there lives in Tim's building.

"Hello there, Tim," he says as they walk in.

"Hello," says Tim. "I've brought my dad."

Dad orders a calzone and Tim has a pizza from the children's menu. They order drinks. Tim has orange juice and Dad has cola.

Tim doesn't eat the crusts. He leaves them on his plate in a ring. Dad eats every last crumb and finishes all of his cola.

"Not bad at all!" he says, and takes out his wallet.

"Dad wants to pay!" Tim calls out to his friend the waiter.

When they leave the pizza place, it's getting dark.
Dad looks at his watch. Tim knows Dad will have
to go back soon. But not just yet. Tim knows where
they can go first...

Tim and Dad sit together in the library. Dad flicks through a magazine. Tim has a book on his knee. He's going to open it. He doesn't know what time it is – he doesn't want to know. Tim doesn't want Dad's train to leave yet.

The librarian has a ponytail and glasses. Her name is Carol.

"Hello, Tim," she says.

"I want to borrow a book," Tim tells her. "Just me. Not Dad."
He points. "This is my dad.

Tim tucks the book under his arm and they leave together –
Tim and Dad.

"Let's have a snack before I go," says Dad.

So they go into a café nearby. Dad lifts Tim up so he can see what's in the cabinet. "I'll have a doughnut," says Tim. Dad orders coffee and a danish pastry.

It's late when they finish eating. Dad has to catch his
train. As they walk to the station, Dad holds Tim's hand.
Dad's hand is big and Tim's small hand disappears inside it.

When they get to the station, there is still time before the train leaves. "Would you like to see inside the train, Tim?" Dad asks.

"Yes," says Tim.

Dad lifts him up and they climb on board.

There are lots of people inside. Everyone is lifting bags onto racks or hanging up coats and jackets.

"Excuse me," Dad announces to the people in the carriage. "Can I say something?"

Everyone stops and stares at him.

"This is Tim," Dad says. "My son. He's the best son any father could have."

Dad carries Tim back onto the platform. He hugs his son tightly. Then he puts him down and rubs his eyes.

"Goodbye, Tim," Dad says. "We'll see each other again very soon."

When Mum arrives, Dad hurries onto the train. Tim stands on the platform with Mum. They see Dad at the window. Then the train starts to move and Dad waves to Tim.

Tim waves back. As the train pulls out of the station, Dad's hand gets smaller and smaller.

Tim and Mum watch until the train is out of sight. But even though the train is gone, the tracks are still there. And one day soon the train will come back along those tracks. The train will come back with Dad. And they will spend another day together – just Tim and Dad.

First published 2008 by Walker Books Ltd
87 Vauxhall Walk, London SE11 5HJ

2 4 6 8 10 9 7 5 3 1

This book has been typeset in Granjon

Printed in China

British Library Cataloguing in Publication Data:
a catalogue record for this book is available from the British Library

ISBN 978-1-4063-1384-0

www.walkerbooks.co.uk